The koala was small and grey, with huge furry ears and curious, bright black eyes. He clung to the front of Great-Uncle Horace's safari jacket, blinking nervously. Zoe was desperate to cuddle him!

N0668816

Look out for:

The Cuddly Koala

Amelia Cobb

Illustrated by **Sophy Williams**

nosy crow

With special thanks to Natalie Doherty

For Jenna x

First published in the UK in 2015 by Nosy Crow Ltd
The Crow's Nest, 14 Baden Place, Crosby Row
London, SE1 1YW, UK

Nosy Crow and associated logos are trademarks and/or
registered trademarks of Nosy Crow Ltd

Text copyright © Working Partners Ltd, 2014
Illustrations © Sophy Williams, 2014

The right of Working Partners Ltd and Sophy Williams to be identified as the author and
illustrator respectively of this work has been asserted by them in accordance with the Copyright,
Designs and Patents Act 1988.

A CIP catalogue record for this book will be available from the British Library

All rights reserved

ISBN: 978 085763 447 4

This book is sold subject to the condition that it shall not, by way of trade
or otherwise, be lent, hired out or otherwise circulated in any form of
binding or cover other than that in which it is published. No part of this
publication may be reproduced, stored in a retrieval system,
or transmitted in any form or by any means (electronic, mechanical,
photocopying, recording or otherwise) without the prior
written permission of Nosy Crow Ltd.

Printed and bound in Great Britain by Clays Ltd, Elcograf S.p.A.

Papers used by Nosy Crow are made from wood grown in sustainable forests.

14

www.nosycrow.com

Chapter One

Holiday at
the Rescue Zoo

"I'm so excited that it's finally half-term!"
said Zoe Parker, swinging her school bag
happily. "And we get a whole week off
school!"

It was Friday afternoon and school had
just broken up for the half-term holiday.
Zoe was walking home with two of her

friends from her class, Nicola and Jack. Their parents were walking just behind them, chatting.

"I'm excited too!" said Nicola with a smile. "I can't wait to have some time to play with Rex."

Zoe grinned at her friend – Nicola had a new dog and he was very cute and bouncy!

"Yeah, and I'm going to help my dad finish our tree house," Jack said. "Then you can both come over and play in it!"

The three friends laughed as they planned their half-term adventures, but then Zoe remembered their homework. "What are you going to do for your science project?" she asked Nicola and Jack.

That morning Zoe's teacher, Miss

Hawkins, had asked everyone in the class to do a special piece of homework over the break. They had to choose something from the natural world to observe carefully, and then write some notes about whatever they had chosen. Miss Hawkins had asked them to take photographs or draw pictures too. Then, after the break, they each had to explain to the class what they had found out. There was even going to be a prize for the best project!

"I think I'm going to do mine about frogs. There's a pond full of frogs and frogspawn at the bottom of my garden," said Jack.

"I might do mine about wildflowers," said Nicola thoughtfully. "My granny lives near the woods and she knows lots about them. I could ask her to take me for a walk there, and help me take pictures."

"Cool! Those are both really good ideas," Zoe said.

"I bet I know what you're going to do yours on, Zoe!" replied Jack with a grin. "One of the animals at the Rescue Zoo!"

Zoe chuckled. Jack was right! As soon as Miss Hawkins had explained about the project, she had known immediately that she wanted to do hers about an animal. They were her favourite things in the whole world, and she knew more about them than anyone else in her class. The only question was: which animal should she write about? There were hundreds of different creatures at the Rescue Zoo – too many to choose from!

"You're so lucky, Zoe," sighed Nicola as they turned the corner and the carved wooden gates of the Rescue Zoo appeared in front of them.

Zoe smiled at Nicola. She *felt* lucky. She wasn't just a visitor at the zoo – she actually lived there!

Zoe's Great-Uncle Horace was a famous explorer and animal expert, and had started the Rescue Zoo so that all the lost, frightened or injured animals he met on his adventures could have a safe and caring home. He was very wise and kind, and Zoe always looked forward to seeing him whenever he came back to visit – especially because he often brought a new animal back to the zoo with him!

Zoe's mum, Lucy, was the zoo vet, and they lived in a pretty little cottage at the edge of the zoo. That meant that Lucy could help any animal that was poorly, day or night – and Zoe got to spend every spare minute she had with the animals.

"Maybe you can come to the zoo one day during the holiday," Zoe suggested to both her friends. "Why don't you ask your parents? I could show you round all my favourite enclosures! We've got the most beautiful young polar bear, called Snowy – she's adorable. And three snow leopard cubs as well!"

"Really? I would love to!" said Nicola, and Jack nodded eagerly.

As she spoke, there was a funny little squeak from just beyond the gate, and a tiny face with big, golden eyes peeped around it. "Meep!" said Zoe. "He must have been waiting for me to get home!"

Nicola and Jack both laughed as Meep
scampered out through
the gate and leaped
into Zoe's arms for
a cuddle. He was a
grey mouse lemur
with a long curly tail,
and so small that he
could perch on Zoe's
shoulder, or fit snugly
inside her pocket! He
was Zoe's best friend, and
had arrived at the Rescue Zoo when
he was a tiny baby. He'd needed lots of
special care, so Zoe and Lucy had taken
him back to their cottage to look after
him – and he'd lived with them there
ever since.

"He's so cute!" cooed Nicola.

Meep wriggled in Zoe's arms until his tummy was exposed, and Zoe giggled. "He'd like you to give his tummy a stroke or a tickle," Zoe told her friends.

Nicola and Jack reached out carefully and tickled Meep. The little lemur gave a happy squeal. "I think he's enjoying that!" laughed Jack.

"Yes, I am!" squeaked Meep. "I'm so glad you're home from school, Zoe. I've missed you all day!"

Zoe winked at her friend. She knew that Nicola and Jack would only hear funny squeaking sounds from Meep — but she actually understood what he was saying. Living at the Rescue Zoo wasn't the only amazing thing about Zoe. She had a secret — a big secret! When she was little, she had found out that animals can understand people. And most amazingly of all, Zoe had a special ability to understand animals, too!

"Come on, Jack! Time to go home," Jack's dad called, waving. Jack nodded. "Coming, Dad."

"See you again soon, Zoe!" said Nicola.

"Do you really think we could come and visit the zoo over the holiday?" Jack asked Zoe hopefully.

"Definitely!" Zoe promised. "I'll get my mum to give your parents a ring."

As her friends walked off chatting excitedly, Zoe, Meep and Zoe's mum walked through the carved wooden gates into the zoo. Zoe could see that it was very busy, and full of visitors.

"I'd better stop by the zoo hospital

before tea," Lucy told Zoe. "One of the pelicans has a poorly wing, and I want to give him a check-up. There's a snack for you on the kitchen table – and one for Meep, because I know he always tries to share yours!"

Zoe grinned. Meep was tiny but he had a big appetite!

As her mum dashed off down the path, Zoe and Meep headed towards the cottage. "Yum, a special snack all for me!" chattered Meep, rubbing his tummy. "What do you think it will be, Zoe? A banana? Or sunflower seeds? I like those a lot. Or maybe some berries?"

"Maybe it's all three!" suggested Zoe, and giggled at the excited expression on Meep's face. "Now, listen, Meep. I need your help. I can't decide what animal to do my science project on! I've got too many ideas and I can't choose one. I could write about the elephants and their long, clever trunks. Or maybe the tigers… Oh, or the leopards, and explain how their patterned coats camouflage them. Or maybe a project about the Rescue Zoo bees, and how they make honey?"

"*Or* you could write all about me,"
Meep said helpfully. "I'm a *very* interesting
animal, Zoe. I have a long, curly tail that
helps me balance when I climb up trees."
He waggled his tail, tickling Zoe's nose
with it. "And I have big eyes that can
see really well in the dark," he added,
widening his eyes at her. Zoe chuckled.
"*And* Goo says I'm one of the smallest
primates in the world," he finished, using
the funny nickname he had for Great-
Uncle Horace, because he found the long
name hard to say.

Zoe laughed again and stroked the little
lemur's head. "You're right, Meep. You are
very interesting!" she agreed. "But I still
don't think I can do my project on you.
Lots of my school friends know about
you already, because I talk about you so

much! I think I need to pick an animal that's a bit different." She sighed. "I wish Great-Uncle Horace was here – he'd help me choose. He's been away for ages now and I really miss him."

As they reached the cottage door, Meep's ears suddenly pricked up. "Zoe, what's that?" he said.

Zoe looked round. "I can't hear anything, Meep."

"It's a funny thudding sound," Meep explained. "It's a bit like when the elephants walk along with their big, heavy feet – but it's much faster."

Zoe could hear the sound now too – and it was quickly getting louder and louder. She looked up at the sky and saw a small blue shape, getting closer every second.

"Zoe, look!" squealed Meep, pointing at the shape with his tiny finger. "Is it a strange kind of bird? It's very big – and very fast!"

Zoe shook her head and smiled. "Meep, I know what it is. It's not a bird – it's a helicopter!"

Chapter Two
A Double Surprise

Zoe slipped the key to the cottage back into her coat pocket and dashed along the zoo path, running as quickly as she could towards the loud thundering sound.

"It looks like the helicopter's going to land in the clearing in front of the gift shop," she called to Meep, who was racing

along beside her, his tiny paws moving so
fast they were almost a blur. Meep seemed
to have forgotten all about his snack. He
was desperate to see what was happening,
just like Zoe!

All around them, the zoo visitors were
looking up at the sky and pointing at the
blue helicopter – and the animals were
getting into a state of excitement too.
Zoe passed a troop of
screeching monkeys,
rhinos stomping
their huge feet and
bellowing noisily,
and parrots who
had fluttered
right to the
tops of their trees
to see better.

"I don't know what's going on yet, Bertie!" Zoe shouted to the zoo's eager little elephant, who was holding his trunk high up in the air and trumpeting curiously. "Meep and I are going to find out!"

As they ran into the clearing, the helicopter was landing on to the grass. Now Zoe could make out a picture painted on the side: a hot-air balloon. This was the special symbol of the Rescue Zoo, and that meant the helicopter could only belong to one person.

"It's Great-Uncle Horace!" Zoe cried. "He's back!"

The blades of the helicopter spun round once more and then stopped, and the door burst open. First, out flew a beautiful bird with sapphire-blue feathers.

It was Kiki, Great-Uncle Horace's macaw, who travelled everywhere with him. Then a smiling face with untidy white hair, a battered old explorer's hat and a pair of twinkling brown eyes popped out.

"Zoe!" Great-Uncle Horace called across the clearing. "Just the person I wanted to see."

As Zoe ran to the helicopter, her mind started whirring. When Great-Uncle Horace came back to the Rescue Zoo, it was usually because he had found another animal that needed a home. Was the Rescue Zoo's newest member inside the helicopter? Zoe really hoped so!

Reaching Great-Uncle Horace, Zoe jumped up to give him a big hug. "You've been away for ages this time," she said. "I'm so happy you're home."

"So am I, my dear!" replied Great-Uncle Horace, swinging her around. "I've been away so long because I've been somewhere that's a long, long way away. In fact, I've almost been to the other side of the world! Can you guess?"

Zoe thought, trying hard to picture

19

the huge map of the world that Miss
Hawkins had pinned up on her classroom
wall. "I think so," she said. "Have you
been to Australia?"

"Exactly right!" said Great-Uncle
Horace, beaming. "I've been to a place
called Queensland. It's almost ten
thousand miles away, Zoe! The funniest
thing about Australia is that their seasons
are the opposite of ours. So when we
are having summer, they're having
winter. And when it's spring in Australia,
it's autumn here. That means that on
Christmas Day, while we're wearing
lots of warm woolly clothes, people in
Australia are having a barbecue on
the beach!"

Zoe laughed. "That's so funny. I can't
imagine a hot and sunny Christmas Day!"

"Now, where was I?" muttered Great-Uncle Horace thoughtfully, and Zoe giggled. "Ah, I know! Surprises!" he cried, reaching into the helicopter and pulling out a brightly wrapped parcel. "I've brought you two surprises from Australia, Zoe. This is the first."

"Thank you!" Zoe turned the present over in her hands, trying to guess what it could be. It was a strange shape, long and curved, a bit like a big, flat banana. Meep was bouncing impatiently on her shoulder, squeaking, "Open it, open it!" so she pulled off the wrapping paper. It was a piece of dark, shiny wood, carved with tiny pictures of people and animals. Zoe thought she recognised it from films she had watched, but she wasn't sure what it was called.

"It's a boomerang!" explained Great-Uncle Horace. "Boomerangs have been made in Australia for thousands of years. Look at the special way the wood is shaped, Zoe – that's so that when you throw it, it will spin round and come right back to you!"

"Really?" asked Zoe, looking at the boomerang.

"Try it!" suggested Great-Uncle Horace. "Just get ready to catch it."

Zoe lifted the boomerang up, raised

22

her arm back and threw it. She watched it sail through the air – and laughed in delight as it spun round and flew neatly back to her. Meep almost fell off her shoulder as he ducked to get out of the boomerang's way!

"And now I think it's time for the second surprise," said Great-Uncle Horace with a smile. "Like the boomerang, I've brought it all the way from Australia – and it's something else that Australia is very famous for."

Zoe held her breath as Great-Uncle Horace reached inside the helicopter and pulled out a wooden crate, fastened with shiny silver buckles. He put the crate carefully on the ground and began to open it. Kiki fluttered down to land on his shoulder as he did so, and Meep clung to Zoe's shoulder, craning his head to try and get a better look.

Great-Uncle Horace lifted the lid off the crate with a smile, and Zoe gasped. "It's a baby koala!"

Chapter Three
Koala Cuddles

"That's right!" said Great-Uncle Horace, reaching inside the crate and lifting the little creature out. "Baby koalas are called joeys, and this little chap is just eight months old."

The koala was small and grey, with furry ears and curious, bright black eyes.

He clung to the front of Great-Uncle Horace's safari jacket with his long claws, blinking nervously. Zoe was desperate to cuddle him! "Why did you bring him back to the Rescue Zoo?" she asked, reaching out and stroking the joey's soft grey head.

"When I was in Queensland, an old friend of mine asked me to pay her a visit. She works at an animal sanctuary there," Great-Uncle Horace explained. "This little fellow had just grown big enough to live outside his mother's pouch, but sadly she abandoned him."

Zoe stared at Great-Uncle Horace. "What? That's awful. Why would she do that?"

Great-Uncle Horace nodded. "It *is* very sad but I'm afraid it's quite common with koalas. They are rather solitary creatures, and like to live alone, so many mothers leave their babies to fend for themselves as soon as they can. That means this joey needed lots of extra-special care – which is why my old friend thought of me! She knew the koala enclosure at Rescue Zoo is a truly amazing place, and thought we might be able to give the joey a good home. Of course, I said yes!"

"It's perfect," said Zoe, thinking of the beautiful enclosure next to the flamingos. It was a tall forest of eucalyptus trees, with a little stream winding through it. "And he'll have a friend – Matilda!" Matilda was the koala who already lived at the zoo.

Great-Uncle Horace nodded. "That's right, although they probably won't spend

very much time together. It's not that
koalas aren't friendly animals, but they do
like their own company and space. Even
so, I'm sure Matilda will help our little
newcomer to feel at home."

"Uncle Horace!" cried a voice from
across the clearing.

Zoe turned and saw her mum rushing
towards them. Like Zoe, Lucy had dark
curly hair, but she usually wore it in a
bun or a ponytail – but right now she
was running so fast it had come loose. "I
saw the helicopter and knew it was you!"
she said breathlessly, reaching up to kiss
her uncle's cheek. "Zoe and I have really
missed you! What's this you've brought
with you – a koala!"

"Yes! Isn't he gorgeous?" said Zoe.

"Oh, he's adorable," said Lucy, stroking

his head. "And so small!"

"I was just explaining to Zoe how I found the little chap." Great-Uncle Horace started to tell the story, then paused and looked at Lucy carefully. Zoe glanced at her mum too, and saw that her face had fallen. "Is something the matter, my dear? You look worried," said Great-Uncle Horace.

"I've just remembered that Kieran is on holiday this week," Lucy explained. Kieran was the zookeeper who looked after Matilda and the other marsupials, including the kangaroos and wallabies. "Some of the other keepers are helping to cover his jobs while he's away, but of course they all have their own enclosures and animals to look after most of the time. A joey like this needs lots of special attention – especially one who's only just arrived and might be feeling a little unsettled. I'm worried that no one will have enough time to take care of him properly. I would help if I could, but I'm so busy at the moment – three of the chipmunks are poorly, and a monkey fell and broke his leg last week. . ."

Great-Uncle Horace looked down at the koala snuggled up in his arms, a concerned frown on his face. But suddenly Zoe had an idea.

"I know!" she burst out. "What if I looked after him? I'm on my school holidays now, so I could take care of the joey until Kieran gets back next week. I already know a little bit about koalas, because I've helped him with Matilda before. And I've looked after brand-new baby animals too, so I'm used to feeding them at funny times." Her eyes lit up as she thought of something else. "And," she added, "this would be perfect for my school project!"

"What school project, Zoe?" asked Great-Uncle Horace.

Zoe quickly explained what she had to do. "I can make lots of notes about the joey's behaviour, and what he likes to eat, and exactly what he looks like. I think Miss Hawkins would love that – plus, I can give all the notes to Kieran when he gets back, so he'll know everything there is to know about the joey!"

"I'm not sure, Zoe," said Lucy. "Looking after an animal all by yourself is a big responsibility, especially a baby."

"She doesn't have to do it all by herself," said Great-Uncle Horace. "I'll be there to help too. We can do it together!"

Zoe beamed at him, and Great-Uncle Horace winked back.

"Well. . ." Lucy hesitated.

"Please say yes, Mum!" begged Zoe, and even Meep crossed his tiny fingers hopefully.

Lucy smiled. "As long as you promise to ask me, Great-Uncle Horace or one of the other zookeepers for help if you get stuck – then yes, I think we can give it a try. I can see how much this means to you, Zoe, and I know you'll work really hard."

"Yay!" cried Zoe, jumping up to give her mum a big hug. "Thanks, Mum! I won't let you down."

Lucy hugged Zoe back. "You're going to be busy!" she said. "The joey will need to be hand-fed something called pap until he's a little bit older.

33

Then he'll move on to eucalyptus, so you'll need to introduce him to the trees in his enclosure, and try to interest him in the leaves."

Great-Uncle Horace smiled. "We'll also encourage him to start climbing! It's wonderful exercise for a koala and will keep his claws in tip-top condition. If they're strong and healthy, that will help this little fellow to grip tree trunks and move up and down them easily," he added, nodding at the joey's small grey paws and curved black claws. "Climbing is very important for koalas, because that's how they find their own leaves to eat and take care of themselves."

Zoe was starting to feel a little bit dizzy – there was so much to remember! But she also felt very excited. She was going to look after a gorgeous baby koala for a whole week! On her shoulder, Meep was hopping up and down. "I'll help too, I'll help too!" he chattered in Zoe's ear.

"I think the first thing to do is learn how to hold the joey properly," suggested Great-Uncle Horace. "Why don't I pass him over to you now, Zoe? Make a cradle with your arms – that's it."

Zoe bent her arms as if she was rocking a baby to sleep, which was the way Great-Uncle Horace had taught her to hold smaller animals like this one. An excited smile crossed her face as Great-Uncle Horace gently passed the joey to her. The little koala snuggled up against her immediately. "He's quite heavy, isn't he!" Zoe said, surprised. "And his fur is so soft and warm."

"Uncle Horace, we'll need to decide where the joey will live until he's ready to move in to his enclosure," said Lucy. "It might be a few weeks before he's climbing by himself and can find his own food. Until then, he'll need feeding by hand several times during the day and night."

As Lucy and Great-Uncle Horace quietly chatted, Zoe moved around so that she was facing away from them and could whisper to the joey without them noticing. "My name is Zoe," she told him, keeping her voice as low as possible. "And this is Meep, my best friend. What's your name?"

The joey looked very surprised to hear Zoe talking – but then he cuddled up to her even tighter. He replied with soft little grunt, and Zoe grinned. "Kipp? It's nice

to meet you,
Kipp," she
whispered,
still
smiling
at him.
"Meep
and I are
going to
look after you
this week."

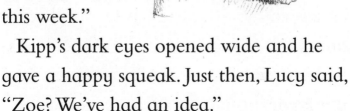

Kipp's dark eyes opened wide and he gave a happy squeak. Just then, Lucy said, "Zoe? We've had an idea."

"The joey can live at Higgins Hall with me until he's ready to live in the koala enclosure," explained Great-Uncle Horace. "Koalas are nocturnal animals, Zoe, which means they like to be active and awake at night – so tonight we'll have a sleepover! We can take it in turns to stay up late, feeding and looking after this little fellow. What do you think?"

"I think that's a brilliant idea. And I *love* sleepovers!" cried Zoe, and Meep leaped down from her shoulder and somersaulted excitedly on the ground. A sleepover at Higgins Hall! Zoe couldn't think of a more fun place to spend the night than the huge, grand house overlooking the zoo. It had belonged to Great-Uncle Horace's family for hundreds of years, and had vast kitchens, a library and even a ballroom. But Great-Uncle Horace had turned almost all of the rooms into homes for different animals, keeping just the attic for himself and Kiki. There was always something interesting to see, no matter which door you opened.

"We'll have to find you a spare bedroom somewhere," Great-Uncle Horace said thoughtfully. "But the animals have taken over almost every nook and cranny of the Hall. . ."

"Why don't we dig out your sleeping bag?" suggested Lucy. "You could camp, Zoe!"

Zoe's eyes lit up. "That would be so much fun! Please can I do that, Great-Uncle Horace?"

"An excellent idea! We'll set your

sleeping bag up in the butterfly room,"
Great-Uncle Horace told Zoe, smiling.
"I know that's your favourite room at
the Hall, my dear. It's certainly one of
the prettiest. You might not get very
much sleep though, because the joey will
need lots of care and attention! And I'll
make sure we have plenty of delicious
snacks. Let me see: strawberry ice cream,
popcorn, and hot chocolate to drink.
And of course, lots of custard creams!"
he added happily. Custard cream biscuits
were Great-Uncle Horace's favourite
things to eat, and he always kept a big
supply at the Hall.

Zoe grinned, and Kipp gave a happy
little grunt. Of course, Great-Uncle
Horace and Lucy didn't know that the
joey had understood everything they had

just said – and now he was excited about
the sleepover, too!

"I'll take him to the zoo hospital now,
to give him a quick check-up," Lucy said,
gently taking Kipp from Zoe. The little
koala gave a whimper as she did, and
held his paws out towards Zoe, but she
nodded encouragingly at him.

"He's very attached to you already, love!" laughed Lucy. "Why don't you go back to the cottage and start getting your bag packed for tonight? I'll walk you over to the Hall after we've had tea."

"And I'll see you soon!" said Great-Uncle Horace.

As Zoe walked back to the cottage, she couldn't stop herself from grinning. "I can't wait for tonight, Meep," she told her little friend, who was scampering along next to her.

"And I can't wait to start my school project either. I never imagined it would be so much fun!"

Chapter Four
Sleepover Time

"Toothbrush, pillow . . . I think I've nearly got everything," said Zoe, looking around her bedroom. "Now I just need my pyjamas. Which ones shall I take, Meep?"

There was a little squeak from inside Zoe's wardrobe and Meep poked his tiny head around the door. "I know! Your blue ones with the kangaroos on them. They might make Kipp feel more at home, Zoe, because kangaroos are from Australia too!"

"Good idea, Meep!" said Zoe, chuckling. She found the pyjamas and stuffed them into her bag, and then they rushed downstairs to the kitchen, where Zoe's mum was waiting.

"Would you like me to walk over to the Hall with you, love?" Lucy offered.

Zoe shook her head. "No, it's OK. I know you need to get back to the zoo hospital. I'll be fine!"

Lucy gave Zoe a big hug. "All right. Well, have lots of fun, and remember to ring me if you and Great-Uncle Horace are having any problems with the joey. And I'll see you in the morning."

Zoe and Meep walked through the zoo to Higgins Hall together. All the visitors had gone home for the day and the zoo gates were shut. The paths were quiet, and that meant Zoe could stop and chat to her animal friends along the way. "I'm going for a sleepover at the Hall!" she explained to the curious parrots, who called out to her in noisy squawks,

wondering what she was carrying a big overnight bag for. "It's so I can help look after the new baby koala, Kipp. I'm so excited!"

"And I'm going to help too!" added Meep importantly.

When they arrived at the Hall, Zoe
pushed open the huge, grand front door
and stepped straight inside. It was always
so noisy in the Hall, because of all the
squeaking and squawking of the different
animals and birds who lived there, so Zoe
knew that if she knocked on the door or
rang the doorbell, Great-Uncle Horace
wouldn't hear it anyway!

"Great-Uncle Horace, I'm here!" she
called, walking through the hallway.
The walls were covered in old paintings
of Great-Uncle Horace's ancestors, all
of them dressed in funny old-fashioned
clothes, and Zoe smiled to see dozens of
cute little hummingbirds perched along
the tops of the picture frames. They all
chirped eagerly at her as she passed them,
and she whispered back, "I know, isn't it

exciting? I love sleepovers!"

"Zoe, is that you?" called Great-Uncle
Horace's voice. "Oh, good! I'm in the
kitchen. Why don't you roll out your
sleeping bag, and then come and join me
in here?"

Zoe carried her things into the butterfly
room. Great-Uncle Horace had cleared a
space for her in a cosy corner, and piled
up extra blankets and cushions that he'd
collected from around the Hall, so that
Zoe could make a snug bed for herself.
When she'd finished setting it up, she
headed back to the kitchen.

She had to bite back a giggle when she
walked in – Great-Uncle Horace had
thrown open all the cupboards and was
piling the kitchen table high with snacks
and treats. She spotted at least three

packets of custard cream biscuits! Kipp was clinging to Great-Uncle Horace's front, and he was supporting the little joey with one arm while he arranged their picnic with his spare hand.

Kipp squealed happily when he saw Zoe. "There you are!" said Great-Uncle Horace, beaming at her. "Now, I hope you're hungry because we've got lots of tasty things to eat. What would you like first? Popcorn? Ice cream? We could even build a little fire in the fireplace and toast marshmallows!" He winked at her. "I know you have a sweet tooth like me, my dear!"

Zoe and her uncle tucked into the snacks, with Kipp cuddled up on Great-Uncle Horace's lap. As they ate, they chatted about his adventures in Australia, and how Zoe was getting on at school. Zoe also told Great-Uncle Horace that she'd thought of a name for the joey. Whenever Zoe met a new arrival at the zoo and secretly asked them their name, she had to pretend she had come up with it herself!

"I think we should call him Kipp," she said, giving the little joey a secret smile.

"That's a splendid name," Great-Uncle Horace agreed, nodding enthusiastically. He broke up a custard cream for Kiki to nibble, and shared some of the crumbs with a few interested pelicans that waddled into the room too. When they couldn't eat another bite, Great-Uncle Horace picked up Kipp and then told Zoe to follow him into the library, where he showed her all the things she would need to look after the little koala that night.

"This is pap," he told her, using his spare hand to pick up a bowl full of what looked like wobbly green jelly. "It has lots of the same vitamins and goodness that eucalyptus leaves do, but it's just a little bit easier for a joey to digest than real leaves. Joeys as small as Kipp like to eat very often, because they're growing quickly, and that makes them hungry a lot of the time! So if Kipp finishes this whole bowl, there's lots more pap in the fridge. I also went to the koala enclosure this afternoon and picked some eucalyptus leaves. He might like to *try* one or two, although he shouldn't eat too many just yet."

Zoe nodded. "And where will he sleep?" she asked.

"Just here." Great-Uncle Horace pointed to a small, round, cosy-looking bed next to one of the huge bookcases. It reminded Zoe of the sort of bed a puppy might sleep in. "But as I said before," he continued, "koalas are nocturnal, so I

think he may be awake and ready to play
for most of the night! If that's the case,
you could show him this special climbing
apparatus that I've had brought in."

Great-Uncle Horace nodded to a
wooden post behind Zoe that was almost
as tall as him, with different wooden
platforms and ledges sticking out along
it. "I've been encouraging him to have
a go, but he's much more interested in
cuddles than climbing," he added. "I
think Kipp might be scared of being
abandoned again, after his mother left
him. So it's even more
important that we
get him climbing
soon – because if
Kipp becomes used to
being carried around

as a baby, and never learns to climb by himself, he'll never be able to find his own food and live a happy, healthy koala lifestyle."

Zoe nodded. "I understand. Do you want to go first looking after Kipp, or shall I?" she asked hopefully.

Great-Uncle Horace chuckled. "I think *you'd* like to go first, my dear – isn't that right? I'll take a nap now, and I'll be down in a little while to take over. Then it will be your turn to sleep! You must promise to wake me up if you have any problems though."

Zoe promised, and excitedly ran to the butterfly room to get changed into her pyjamas. Then she ran back to the library, gave Great-Uncle Horace a goodnight hug and kiss, and carefully took Kipp from him. Again, Zoe was surprised at how heavy he felt! The little koala gave a happy squeak as he snuggled down in Zoe's arms, but Zoe waited until she heard the door to Great-Uncle Horace's attic bedroom click shut before she spoke to him.

"Meep and I have been really looking forward to seeing you again, Kipp!" she told the joey, giving him a cuddle. "Are you feeling sleepy yet?"

The joey shook his little head firmly, his eyes bright and wide awake, and Zoe giggled. "You definitely don't seem sleepy! OK then, Kipp – would you like to try climbing? We've got this brilliant climbing frame for you to practise on," she added, turning Kipp round so he could see it.

"Or maybe you're hungry?" suggested Meep helpfully.

Kipp gave an eager squeak, and Zoe laughed. "OK, Kipp – let's feed you," she replied. "Great-Uncle Horace told us all about this special mixture."

She sat in Great-Uncle Horace's comfiest armchair, with Meep perched on her shoulder. Kipp was nestled in one arm, and Zoe held the bowl of pap in her other hand. She secretly thought it looked a bit strange, but Kipp squealed excitedly when he saw it, and gobbled the whole lot down. Then Zoe offered him a eucalyptus leaf. He gave it a curious sniff, then nibbled it happily. "Wow, you really were hungry!" exclaimed Zoe when he was finished, patting the joey's full tummy. "Maybe now you'd like to have a go at climbing?"

But the little koala gave a happy sigh and cuddled up against Zoe even more tightly. Great-Uncle Horace was right – Kipp wasn't interested in climbing when he could cuddle instead! Zoe giggled at how snug and cute he was, but she remembered what Great-Uncle Horace had warned her about.

"Meep, it's really important that Kipp starts to learn how to climb," she whispered. "Great-Uncle Horace would be so pleased if Kipp had already had a go by the time he came back downstairs!"

Meep nodded, and then his big golden eyes lit up. "What if I show him how, Zoe?" the little lemur suggested. "I'm good at climbing!"

"That's a great idea, Meep!" said Zoe. "Kipp, watch Meep! Don't you think it looks fun?"

Meep scampered over to the bottom of the climbing post and turned to make sure the joey was watching him. Then

he leaped lightly up the post to the first
wooden platform, hopped up to the next,
and scurried the rest of the way. At the
very top he balanced on one paw and
pulled a funny face. "Easy peasy!" he
squeaked.

Kipp looked interested, and held out his
little paws towards the post. Zoe put him
down carefully at the bottom and showed
him how to use his claws to grip the
wood. "That's it!" she said encouragingly,
as Kipp slowly moved his right paw up
the post. "Now do the same with your left
paw."

But Kipp wouldn't go any higher. He
stopped where he was and squealed
anxiously to get down. "OK, Kipp, don't
worry. I'm coming," Zoe reassured him,
rushing to pick him up again. "There –

I've got you! That was a really good start, Kipp. I'm very proud of you for giving it a try."

Kipp clung tightly to her front and buried his little face against her pyjamas. Zoe felt a pang of worry. "Meep, I think this is going to be harder than I'd first thought," she whispered to her friend, who was still sitting on her shoulder. "We'll try again tomorrow. We've got to do everything we can to get Kipp climbing!"

Just a few hours later, Great-Uncle Horace came down to look after Kipp, yawning sleepily. Meep giggled when he saw Great-Uncle Horace's pyjamas: they were bright orange and covered in little zebras!

"Well well, our little friend looks happy!" he said, beaming at Kipp, who was trying another eucalyptus leaf. "You must have done a splendid job, Zoe. Now, it's time for you to get some rest. Go and get comfy in your sleeping bag."

Zoe nodded. This was the latest she had ever stayed up before, and she was feeling really sleepy, although she was sad to leave Kipp when they'd been having so much fun! Great-Uncle Horace seemed to guess what she was thinking, because he added, "Don't worry, my dear – it will be morning before you know it, and then you'll see Kipp again."

Zoe and Meep were both yawning by the time they reached the butterfly room. As Zoe pushed the door open there was a gentle rustling sound, like someone walking through autumn leaves: all the butterflies stirring.

"Sorry! I didn't mean to wake you up," Zoe whispered. "We'll try to be really quiet."

She left the light off and they tiptoed across to her sleeping bag in the dark, trying not to disturb the butterflies any more. Zoe wriggled inside first, and Meep curled up into a little ball on her pillow. It was warm, cosy and quiet, and they quickly fell asleep with the peaceful fluttering sound of butterfly wings all around them.

Zoe woke up to a funny, soft tickling against her nose and cheeks, and opened her eyes to see a pretty green butterfly fluttering against her face. Sunshine was streaming through the windows.

"Good morning!" she whispered to the butterfly. "Thanks for waking me up!"

Great-Uncle Horace was frying eggs and buttering toast in the kitchen, with Kipp perched in a basket on the kitchen table. "Good morning, my dear!" he called when he saw Zoe. "Did you sleep well? After breakfast we'll head straight to the koala enclosure. I'd like us to start introducing Kipp to his new home as early as possible, even if he's not quite ready to live there just yet. I think this little fellow missed you," he added, chuckling. As soon as Kipp saw Zoe and

Meep, he squeaked "hello" eagerly, and Zoe whispered "hello" back when Great-Uncle Horace's back was turned.

When they'd eaten, they got dressed and headed off. Because it was the school holidays, the Rescue Zoo was already bustling with visitors by the time Zoe and Great-Uncle Horace made their way along the path to the koala enclosure. Kipp was cuddled in Zoe's arms, Meep scampered along next to them and Kiki fluttered overhead. Lots of visitors gasped when they saw such a funny group wandering along, and Zoe felt proud when she heard one girl say, "Mum, that girl is allowed to hold the animals! Do you think she's a proper zookeeper?"

Lucy was waiting for them at the koala enclosure, and smiled when she saw them arriving. "How was your sleepover, love?" she asked, kissing Zoe on the forehead. "I missed you!"

"It was really fun – and I've got lots to write about for my project already!" Zoe told her. "Kipp loved the pap we gave him, and he tried a few leaves too. He hasn't got the hang of climbing yet though, but I want to try again today."

"It sounds like you've been working really hard. Well done, Zoe," said Lucy. "Now, do you want to carry Kipp into the enclosure?"

Zoe nodded. "I hope he likes it," she said.

Lucy held the gate open for them, and Zoe carried Kipp inside. She walked all the way around the enclosure with Kipp in her arms, whispering to him whenever she felt sure that her mum and Great-Uncle Horace couldn't hear her. "This will be a lovely bed for you to sleep in," she explained quietly. "And look at all these tall trees! They're perfect for you to practise your climbing – and if you manage to go a little bit higher today, I'll pick the biggest, juiciest eucalyptus leaf I can find for you, as a reward!"

Kipp loved the enclosure and squeaked a shy hello when he saw Matilda, the other koala he would be sharing his new home with – but he still didn't seem ready to start climbing. Zoe put him down gently at the bottom of a tree and he crept towards it, sniffing curiously, but paused when he got closer. "Go on, Kipp!" she whispered encouragingly.

"Zoe?" called Lucy. "I've got to go back

to the zoo hospital now so I'll see you at the cottage for lunch, OK? Great-Uncle Horace is going to stay with you, in case you need any help."

"OK!" replied Zoe, waving. "Oh, Mum, before you go, please can I borrow your phone? I want to use the camera on it to take some pictures of Kipp for my project."

"Of course!" said Lucy, passing Zoe her phone. Zoe snapped a few shots of Kipp, and then of the tree he was standing next to. Just as Lucy left the enclosure, Zoe heard another set of footsteps approaching – and then a cross voice. "What is going on here?"

Zoe groaned quietly. Mr Pinch! The moany old zoo manager was always complaining, and she just knew he would

be unhappy when he found out that Zoe
was looking after Kipp. He thought Zoe
and Meep were a nuisance around the
zoo, and had told Zoe before that only
"real, grown-up zookeepers" should be
allowed to help with the animals. She
thought this was very unfair.

Mr Pinch strode into the enclosure,
looking suspicious. His uniform was
spotless as usual, and his shoes and hat
polished to a shine. Mr Pinch hated mess!

"I heard from some of the keepers that
we had a new koala - and that you are
looking after him. *By yourself*," he told
Zoe sternly.

Great-Uncle Horace burst in quickly.
"Oh, Zoe isn't doing it alone, Percy," he
reassured Mr Pinch. "The two of us are
caring for the joey together. We make an

excellent team!"

Mr Pinch frowned. "Well, I'm still not very happy about this. We have lots of *proper* zookeepers who could do it."

As Great-Uncle Horace began to explain how busy everyone was, Zoe heard an excited little squeak from behind her. She turned round and gasped. While she had been listening to Mr Pinch, Kipp had plucked up the courage to try climbing the eucalyptus tree after all. To Zoe's surprise, he was perched halfway up it, even higher than Zoe's head, gripping the trunk with his strong claws. And he wanted Zoe to see!

Meep was bouncing up and down eagerly. "Kipp's climbing! Kipp's climbing!" the little lemur chattered.

"I can't believe it!" said Zoe.

But as she watched, she saw the expression on the little joey's face quickly change. He looked down and realised how far from the ground he

was. Suddenly his
squeaks became
frightened.
He wanted to
come down
right away – but
he didn't know
how!

Zoe stared at the
little koala in panic.
She didn't know what
to do! She wanted to call
out to Kipp and tell him
to stay still, and that she
and Great-Uncle Horace
would help him climb back
down. But she couldn't talk to him
with Great-Uncle Horace and Mr Pinch
standing right there. Zoe couldn't risk

them finding out about her secret ability.

Feeling as though her feet were frozen, Zoe watched in horror as Kipp tried wriggling back down the trunk. But he lost his grip – and fell all the way to the ground!

Chapter Five
The Poorly Koala

Zoe rushed over to the poor little koala, with Great-Uncle Horace and Mr Pinch right behind her. Very carefully, she scooped him into her arms. Kipp's nose twitched anxiously and he was shaking. Zoe could tell he had hurt himself.

"I'd better take him straight to Mum,"

she told Great-Uncle Horace, who nodded worriedly.

"I told you this was a bad idea," Mr Pinch muttered, shaking his head.

Zoe rushed to the zoo hospital, her heart pounding. It was all her fault that Kipp had fallen! Why hadn't she been watching him more carefully? She felt so upset that she couldn't even stop to answer her animal friends who called out to her along the way, wanting to know what was wrong.

She burst through the zoo hospital doors, breathlessly calling, "Mum! Mum!"

"I'm here, Zoe!" replied Lucy, coming out of her office. When she saw Zoe cradling the trembling joey, her expression became very serious. "What's wrong? What happened?"

Almost in tears, Zoe explained.

"Let's take a look at him," said Lucy, gently taking Kipp from Zoe and examining his furry head, arms and legs, and all four paws. When she touched his left leg, Kipp squeaked miserably, and Lucy examined it more carefully. Finally she sighed. "Nothing's broken, thank goodness. His leg is little bit grazed, and it will be sore for a few days. I'll give him some medicine to stop it hurting as much, and wrap it in a bandage. Then he'll need to rest."

Zoe nodded. She was relieved that Kipp hadn't hurt himself more seriously – but she still felt really guilty. Even so, she couldn't believe it when her mum said gently, "Zoe, I think it would be for the best if you found another animal to write your school project on."

"Mum!" gasped Zoe. "Please, it was an accident. I know I should have watched him more carefully, but I promise I won't let him out of my sight from now on."

Lucy nodded. "I know it was an accident, love, and I'm sorry. But a brand-new baby animal is so much responsibility, and I think it's a bit much for you. And wouldn't it be easier to write about an animal you know really well already, anyway – Bertie the elephant, or Rory the lion cub?"

Zoe didn't know what to say. She loved both Bertie and Rory, of course – but she had been so excited about helping to look after Kipp, and writing her project on him. Now she had ruined it. "Can I still see him?" she asked in a very small voice.

"Of course you can, love," said Lucy, hugging Zoe. "Please don't be upset. I know you worked really hard and did your best. Great-Uncle Horace told me what a good job you did at the Hall last night! The other zookeepers will pitch in and help to look after him, and I'm sure you'll still be able to visit and help out."

When Lucy went into another room to fetch Kipp's medicine and a bandage, Zoe rushed over to the little joey, who squealed anxiously at her. "Kipp, I'm so sorry," she told him. "I feel awful! Does your leg hurt really badly?"

But Kipp didn't seem to mind about his leg. He was more upset that Zoe wouldn't be able to look after him any more! He nuzzled his little head against her, squeaking sadly.

Zoe stroked his furry head. "It's not your fault," she said. "You weren't being clumsy. You mustn't think that! It's all my fault."

As she heard her mum coming back into the room, she dropped her voice to a whisper. "Listen, Kipp – I promise I'll think of a way to look after you again. I don't know how, but I'll come up with something!"

Three days later, Zoe went back to the zoo hospital with Meep to visit Kipp. She had tried to keep busy around the zoo, helping to feed the penguins and clean out the giraffe enclosure. Nicola and Jack had come to the zoo for the day, and she had shown them all the different animal enclosures, which her friends had loved.

But the whole time she had been thinking and worrying about the little joey and his poorly leg. She felt so guilty about his accident.

"Hi, love," called Lucy as Zoe popped her head round the door. "Come in! Your little friend is doing much better today."

"Is his leg getting better?" Zoe asked anxiously, walking over to where her mum was unwrapping the bandage from the joey's leg. Kipp squealed happily up at her, pleased to see her again.

"It's almost completely healed!" Lucy said. "That's the good news. There's some bad news though, I'm afraid."

Zoe looked at her mum. "What? What's wrong?"

Lucy sighed. "Kipp's fall seems to have made him even more nervous – not just

81

about climbing but even being carried around," she explained. "Jess, Frankie and some of the other zookeepers have taken him into the koala enclosure several times this week to try and encourage him to have another go. As well as building his confidence back up, climbing would exercise his leg and help it to heal quicker. But he just clings to the keepers and won't let go. It's as if he's frightened that they're going to drop him."

Lucy sighed and stroked the koala's furry head, looking worried. "They all love cuddling him, of course," she added. "But the problem is, he's getting bigger and heavier every day, and it's becoming really hard for them to carry him all the time, especially when they have other animals they need to take care of."

"Mum, could I have another go at looking after him?" Zoe asked hopefully. She felt sure that if she could speak to Kipp privately, she'd be able to convince him to climb again!

But Lucy looked unsure. "I don't know, Zoe," she said. "I know how carefully you'd look after him. But Mr Pinch saw Kipp fall the other day, remember. He's still very cross about it. If he knew that you were taking care of Kipp again, he'd make a fuss. Now, I think it's time for Kipp to have a nap – he's had a very tiring few days and he still needs to rest."

As her mum carried Kipp into the next room to settle him down for his nap, Zoe and Meep huddled together.

"Zoe, what shall we do?" chattered Meep. "Shall we come back in secret tonight and talk to Kipp when there's no one around?"

Zoe shook her head. "If Mum finds out, we'll be in even more trouble," she whispered. "But we do need to think of a plan, Meep. We need to help Kipp climb again!"

Later that day Zoe and Meep were sitting on a bench outside the zoo café. Zoe was trying to work on her school science project, but it was hard now that she couldn't write about Kipp any more. She couldn't decide what to do instead, and all she had managed to write so far was her name at the top of the page.

Naughty Meep was restless, and was not being very helpful. First he had nibbled the corner of Zoe's exercise book, and then he'd knocked her pencil case on to the floor, scattering her pens and pencils everywhere.

"Meep, are you chewing my red felt tip now?" asked Zoe with a frown. "You've got red ink all over your face. You look like you're wearing lipstick, you cheeky thing!"

Meep scampered up on to her shoulder and cuddled against her neck. "I'm bored, Zoe," the tiny lemur complained.

Zoe sighed. "And I just keep thinking about Kipp," she said. "I wish Mum would let us look after him again. And I wish he wasn't growing so quickly! If he was climbing by himself, it wouldn't matter. But because all the zookeepers are having to carry him around everywhere, it's a big problem. He's getting too heavy for any of them to hold him for long, and they have other jobs to do."

"It's a pity he's not tiny and light like me," chattered Meep.

Zoe cuddled Meep. "I wonder if we

can think of a way to make it easier for the zookeepers to carry him?" she said thoughtfully. "Then Kipp could build his confidence back up slowly, and try climbing again when he feels ready."

Meep wrinkled up his little nose in concentration. "Maybe Goo can help?" he suggested.

"I think I have an even better idea," said Zoe. "Let's go back to the koala enclosure and talk to Matilda! She might have some ideas about how we can help Kipp."

Zoe swept her books and pencil case back into her school bag, threw it over her shoulder and they set off. Five minutes later they arrived at the entrance to the koala enclosure, and Zoe reached for the necklace she was wearing. It was no ordinary necklace – it had been a present

from Great-Uncle Horace, and the
pretty silver paw-print charm
dangling from it opened every
single door or gate in the zoo.
It was Zoe's most special,
precious possession.

Zoe touched the
charm against the gate,
and with a click it
swung open for her.

"Matilda?" called
Zoe as they stepped
inside. "It's us, Zoe
and Meep. We want
to ask your advice!"

She looked around,
but all she could
see were tall, leafy
eucalyptus trees.

Then
there was
a friendly
squeak from
high up above her
head.

"That's Matilda!" said
Zoe. "Meep, will you climb
up the tree and talk to her?"
Meep agreed, looking very
pleased to be asked to do such an
important job. He leaped from Zoe's
shoulder on to the tree trunk and
scurried up it, disappearing into the
leaves at the top. Zoe waited, hearing
the two animals talking in low voices.
Then she heard Meep say, "Thank you!"
and his little face popped through the
leaves again.

"What did Matilda say?" asked Zoe as Meep scampered down and jumped back into her arms.

"I explained the problem," Meep told her. "I said we needed a way to make carrying Kipp easier. Matilda said that in the wild, grown-up koalas carry their babies on their backs."

Zoe nodded. "Yes, I remember seeing pictures of them," she said. "But how can the zookeepers carry Kipp on *their* backs? They're much bigger than a koala. Wouldn't he fall off?"

Meep frowned. "I don't know, Zoe," he admitted.

Zoe cuddled her little friend. "Never mind, Meep. We'll think of something. Come on."

She reached down to grab her school

bag and suddenly stopped, staring at it.
"Meep – I think I might have an idea
after all! Quick – we need to go back to
the cottage!"

Chapter Six
Zoe's Plan

As they rushed through the zoo, Meep wanted Zoe to explain her idea – but Zoe just smiled at her little friend. "Wait and see, Meep," she said. "I think you're going to like it!"

When they reached the cottage, Zoe ran up the stairs to her bedroom and

threw open her wardrobe door. Poor
Meep was more confused than ever!

"Are you getting changed?" he asked.

Zoe laughed as she rummaged around
inside her wardrobe. "I'm looking for
something. I'm sure it's in here. . ." she
called. "Yes – here it is!" She pulled out
a yellow rucksack. "My school bag from
last year. I had to stop using it because
the zip broke – but I kept it, just in case
it came in useful one day. I'm glad I did
now!"

"But what do you need your old school
bag for, Zoe?" Meep wanted to know.

"You'll see very soon," Zoe promised,
scooping him up and dashing back down
the stairs. "Now, we're going over to
Higgins Hall again. We need some help
from Great-Uncle Horace!"

When they reached the Hall, Zoe heard a funny noise coming from inside. "What's that, Meep?" she asked, peeping through a window. "It sounds musical! Is it . . . singing?"

As she pushed open the door, the sound got louder. Now Zoe could make out whistling coming from the kitchen. She peered round the door. Kiki was perched on the kitchen table chirping a tune, and Great-Uncle Horace was humming along cheerily and tapping his feet while he put custard cream biscuits on a plate. Zoe couldn't help giggling, and Great-Uncle Horace looked up.

"Zoe! What a nice surprise," he said. "Come in, come in! How can I help you, my dear? You look as though you're up to something," he added, smiling at Zoe's excited expression.

"I am! I have an idea to help Kipp," Zoe told him, putting her old school bag on the kitchen table in front of him. "He's getting too heavy for the zookeepers to keep carrying around, so I want to turn this rucksack into a special harness for him! It would make him much easier to carry, and it'll mean the zookeepers can keep their hands free for the other stuff they have to do! *And*, if Kipp feels safe, and isn't worrying about being dropped, it should help his confidence. Then he might even start climbing again!"

Great-Uncle Horace picked up the rucksack and looked at it carefully. "I see! You mean something a little bit like a baby sling? Goodness, Zoe, that is an excellent idea. We'll need to cut holes for his arms and legs, and make sure it's comfy enough for him to sit in . . . but yes, I think it could work!"

Zoe was so relieved that Great-Uncle Horace liked her idea. As he found scissors and a needle and thread in a kitchen cupboard, she ran into the library and grabbed a well-worn cushion from one of the chairs. It already had a hole in it, and Zoe brought it back to Great-Uncle Horace.

"Is it OK to use this for Kipp's carrier?"

she asked him.

"Of course! Go ahead," Great–Uncle
Horace replied with a grin.

Great Uncle Horace pulled the squishy

filling out of the cushion, and Zoe sewed
the soft fabric cover inside the rucksack,
so that it would be more comfortable
for Kipp. Then, very carefully, they cut
four arm and leg holes in the rucksack.
Zoe found a blue marker pen and added
the finishing touches. She wrote Kipp's
name in big letters across the front of the
rucksack, and drew little pictures of leaves
around it as decoration.

"There!" said Great-Uncle Horace,
standing back to take a proper look at
their creation. "It looks splendid, Zoe, I
must say. Perhaps we should try it out?"

Great-Uncle Horace helped Zoe put
the rucksack on, and then looked at
Meep. "I wonder if we could persuade
Meep to jump in?" he said. "Perhaps we
should scatter some crumbs or pieces of

fruit inside – I know he has a big appetite
for such a tiny creature. . ."

But Zoe winked at Meep, and
Meep scampered straight into the bag,
disappearing inside. "It's as if he knew just
what we wanted him to do!" said Great-
Uncle Horace, his eyes twinkling, and
Zoe giggled.

Meep was
much smaller
than
Kipp, but
wiggled
right to
the bottom
of the
rucksack
and stuck
one of his little

paws out of a leg hole. "It's very cosy in here, Zoe!" he squeaked.

"I think it's going to work," said Great-Uncle Horace with a satisfied nod. "Well done, Zoe."

"But we still need to make sure it's the right fit for Kipp," said Zoe. "And we need to see if it helps his confidence! Can we go straight to the hospital now?"

"I think that's an excellent idea, my dear," Great-Uncle Horace replied, grabbing his hat. "Let's go!"

They arrived at the zoo hospital just a few minutes later. Lucy was crouched beside Charles, the enormous giant tortoise, listening to his heartbeat through a stethoscope. Charles was the oldest animal in the whole zoo. In fact, he was even older than Great-Uncle Horace!

"Charles has a bit of a cold, but nothing to worry about," Lucy explained to them. "It's been such a busy morning here – a parakeet with a broken wing, a meerkat with a cut paw, and Alex the gorilla has a tummy bug! And poor Kipp is still here," she added, glancing over to where the little joey was huddled sadly.

"Another zookeeper took him over to the koala enclosure this morning, and tried to encourage him to climb again. But Kipp just clung to her, and in the end she had to come back here because he was too heavy to hold for much longer and she had other work she had to do."

"Well, Zoe has had an idea that might help!" Great-Uncle Horace told her. "Zoe, why don't you explain?"

Zoe showed her mum the specially

adapted rucksack, and Lucy listened carefully. "I see no harm in trying it," she said eventually. "I'll put the rucksack on, Zoe, and you lift Kipp inside it. We'll have to make sure it fits properly and that Kipp is comfortable."

As Lucy slipped the straps of the rucksack over her shoulders and knelt down, Zoe went over to pick Kipp up. Very quietly, she whispered to him, "Kipp, I've got an idea to help you – and if it works, I think I'll be allowed to look after you again. But you have to trust me!"

The little joey nodded eagerly at her, and Zoe lifted him inside the rucksack on her mum's back. She gently guided his arms and legs through the holes that Great-Uncle Horace had made in the bag, and then she stood back to take

a look. Zoe waited nervously as Kipp
looked down at the funny sling he was
sitting in. Then he looked up – and gave a
big, happy squeal!

"He likes it!" cried Zoe.

"Hooray!" chirped Meep.

"It's a perfect fit," said Lucy with a huge
smile. "Well done, Zoe."

"Mum," asked Zoe, "would it be OK if I took Kipp over to the koala enclosure, so he can get used to his new sling?"

Lucy smiled. "I think so. You've obviously given so much thought to this, Zoe, and you must really care about Kipp. I'm very proud of you."

Great-Uncle Horace helped to transfer the rucksack from Lucy's back to Zoe's, and then waved them off at the door.

Once they were out of earshot, Zoe turned her head to speak to Kipp. "You look very comfy back there!" she said. "Do you feel nice and secure in your new harness?"

Kipp nodded eagerly and gave a happy squeak. He *loved* his new harness!

"You seem more confident already!" Zoe took a breath, then began again gently. "Listen, Kipp – I would love to see you give climbing another try. I promise that if you take it really slowly, and don't go too high at first, you'll love it. And I'm sure you won't fall again! What do you think?"

Kipp paused for a moment, and Zoe knew he was thinking about his fall the other day. Then he gave a small squeak, and Zoe beamed. "Of course I'll stay with you the whole time," she said. "I'll stand right next to the tree, and if you start to feel frightened, I'll lift you straight down."

Zoe felt so happy as she walked through the zoo, with Kipp snugly nestled against her back and Meep scampering next to her. The other animals thought the rucksack looked brilliant too – and some of them wanted one for themselves!

"I don't think you'd fit into one, Bertie," giggled Zoe as the funny baby elephant trumpeted excitedly. "You're just a bit too big!"

When they got to the koala enclosure, even Matilda came to see the special sling, and squeaked approvingly. "Now, let's just try a very small tree," Zoe suggested to Kipp, who was starting to look nervous again. "Maybe Matilda could show us a good one to start with?"

Matilda gave an eager squeak. She led them through the enclosure to a slender tree that looked younger than most of the others, and had lots of claw-marks along its trunk. "So this was the tree that you learned to climb on, Matilda?" said Zoe, smiling at the koala. "Kipp, this is perfect!"

Zoe helped Kipp out of the rucksack,

and slowly the little joey crept over to the
tree. He gave it a cautious sniff and then
looked at Zoe uncertainly.

"You can do it, Kipp!" said Zoe. "Just
take it nice and steady."

Meep and Matilda made encouraging

squeals too. Kipp took a determined breath, put his front paws against the tree trunk and slowly started climbing.

"That's it! You're doing it, Kipp!" cried Zoe. "We're all right here if you need our help, I promise."

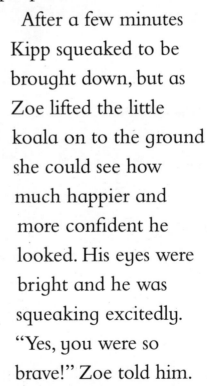

After a few minutes Kipp squeaked to be brought down, but as Zoe lifted the little koala on to the ground she could see how much happier and more confident he looked. His eyes were bright and he was squeaking excitedly. "Yes, you were so brave!" Zoe told him.

"Soon you'll be climbing and playing and picking juicy leaves right at the top of all the highest trees, just like Matilda. And I've got lots to write about for my school project now," she added with grin. "I think Miss Hawkins will love hearing all about you!"

"And you can write about the special harness you made too," Meep chirped. "You might even win the prize!"

"I hope so," replied Zoe. "But the best prize is being able to help my friends like little Kipp here. And thank *you* so much for your help too, Meep," she added, smiling at her best friend. "I feel luckier than ever to live at the Rescue Zoo!"

If you enjoyed Kipp's story,
look out for:

Zoe's Rescue ZOO

The Wild Wolf Pup

Chapter One
A Special School Trip

Zoe Parker rushed excitedly towards the Rescue Zoo gates, followed by her teacher and the rest of the class.

"We're here!" she said happily. "Welcome to the Rescue Zoo, everyone!"

"I still can't believe you actually live here, Zoe," her friend Nicola exclaimed. "You're so lucky."

"I know!" replied Jack, who was walking next to Nicola. "I can't imagine how cool it must be waking up every morning and seeing elephants and giraffes out of your bedroom window!"

Zoe grinned at her friends.

"It's so much fun!" she replied. "I've lived at the Rescue Zoo ever since I was a baby, and sometimes I still can't believe it!"

Zoe's Great-Uncle Horace was a world-famous explorer and animal expert, and he had started the zoo so that any lost, injured or endangered animals he came across on his travels would have a safe and caring home. Zoe's mum, Lucy, was the zoo vet, and Lucy and Zoe lived in a cosy little cottage on the edge of the zoo. Zoe loved animals more than anything, and couldn't imagine living anywhere else. As she and her friends reached the gates, she felt like she might burst with pride.

Zoe had been looking forward to this day for weeks. Halloween was coming up soon, and her class had been learning all about creatures like bats, beetles and spiders. Miss Hawkins had explained that lots of people thought these animals were scary or spooky, but that really there was nothing to be frightened of. Zoe had agreed – they were some of her favourite animals! Now everyone in the class loved them, and when Zoe had mentioned that the Rescue Zoo had a huge spider house, several types of snake and a big family of bats, Miss Hawkins had decided to organise a special class trip to the zoo!

Zoe's class had had normal lessons that morning, and after lunch they had set off together, walking through their town towards the zoo, carefully supervised by their teacher. Zoe couldn't wait to get to the Rescue Zoo – and neither could her friends! Lucy, Zoe's mum, was waiting for them at the entrance. "Hi, everyone!" she said as they walked inside. "You're right on time! I'm so glad you could all make it."

"Thank you for having us!" replied Miss Hawkins, smiling. "Where are we going to start?"

"I thought we'd go to the spider house first, which is over in that direction," said Lucy, pointing. "After that we'll go and see the bats, and, if there's time, the snakes right at the end. Zoe, why don't you lead the way?"

Zoe led her class proudly through the zoo, pointing out her favourite animals to Nicola and Jack as they walked along the path. "That's Leonard and Rory, our lions," she explained. "Well, Rory's a lion cub! And that's the panda enclosure. Chi Chi and Mei Mei are twin sisters, and they came all the way from China. They're really naughty, but so cute!"

Her friends peered into each enclosure, grinning broadly. But when they arrived at the spider house, Zoe spotted a grumpy-looking man waiting outside, wearing a spotless zoo uniform and hat, and holding a broom. "Oh no," she sighed. "Mr Pinch!"

"Who's that?" whispered Nicola. "Does he work here? He looks a bit cross!"

Zoe nodded. "He's the zoo manager," she whispered back. "He's always grumbling or groaning about something – especially mess. He hates it when anything's untidy!"

"I heard your class would be visiting the

zoo today, Zoe," said Mr Pinch. "If you ask me, there is nothing that creates more mess at this zoo than school trips. Always dropping litter and chewing gum and bits of packed lunch everywhere! If I see any mess, I'll know who was responsible." Mr Pinch narrowed his eyes at Zoe and her school friends, then muttered, "It's not as if I don't already have enough to do without sweeping up after you all. Being the zoo manager is a very busy and important job."

"Oh, you won't need to sweep up after us," Miss Hawkins replied firmly. "My class certainly won't be dropping any litter or chewing gum, and they've already had their packed lunches at school."

"Hmmm. Even so, I still think I'd better

supervise," replied Mr Pinch, frowning.

Zoe's mum winked at Zoe and then turned to Mr Pinch. "Oh, there's no need for that, Percy," she said firmly. "I can look after everyone!"

Lucy and Miss Hawkins ushered everyone inside the spider house and Mr Pinch stalked away, muttering crossly to himself...